THE FARM AS IT WAS

Ed Fisher Jr.

THE FARM AS IT WAS

Contact the author at:
16570 Cottonwood Ct, Northville, MI 48168.

Printed in Victoria, BC, Canada.

ISBN: 978-1-4269-1703-5 (sc)

Our mission is to efficiently provide the world's finest, most comprehensive book publishing service, enabling every author to experience success. To find out how to publish your book, your way, and have it available worldwide, visit us online at www.trafford.com

Trafford rev. 11/17/2009

 www.trafford.com

North America & international
toll-free: 1 888 232 4444 (USA & Canada)
phone: 250 383 6864 ♦ fax: 812 355 4082

Dedication

Edward A. Fisher, Jr.

1926 - 2007

W e, his brother, sisters and cousins wish to dedicate, posthumously, this book to Ed with love, gratitude and deep respect for his many artistic and literary gifts. Without him this chronicle of childhood visits to a family farm would not have happened. He was a gifted artist, graphic designer, typographer, illustrator, architect of homes, calligrapher, typographer, writer and educator. An example of his writing imagery appeared in a letter he wrote to his brother where he casually mentioned the trees losing their leaves in the fall.

He wrote, "Outside, the wind is blowing the leaves and they are skittering across the lawn to hide in the woods for the winter."

Pure poetic imagery!

The Farms As It Was

To Begin

This is the true story of a child who grew from toddler to teen during the1930s decade, a city child who regularly spent time with his brother, sister, and cousins on the family farm of their grandparents and an uncle.

The ever-changing mix of people, animals, machines, seasons, and crops was all new to us. Back then, the American Family Farm was facing the economic changes of the Great Depression. Too many farms failed. Then suddenly came the pressures during World War II to produce crops overtime.

During those same years useful technologies beyond the US Mail and the telephone were reaching most rural areas. Electrification of the countryside brought the household conveniences of the city, plus milking machines and electric water pumps. Radio reduced the isolation of farmers and the gasoline engines in tractors and trucks gradually replaced animal power.

We children, of different ages, were witness to some of these changes year by year when we visited the farm of our grandparents. Our daily routines as urban school children were clearly very different from their rural way of life. Our family trips to the farm were filled with many new experiences relished by adventurous kids.

Here is how we remember fondly our early farm visits.

– Ed Fisher jr.

Off To The Farm

We were all of a young age – those years of genuine childhood before the terrible teens set in. Cousins Margaret and Joan from the nearby town and my younger brother Dick and older sister Barbara and I were from 60 miles distant – as distant was in those days of narrow country roads, frequent towns, railroad crossings and many crossroads not yet controlled by traffic lights. Getting there wasn't half the fun; it took our wood-frame Buick sedan almost three hours. And you know how kids can be in cars.

We played road games from the back seat while the parents ran the show from the front. One favorite game was scanning the fields from your own side of the car for horses in the fields and then adding them up. The other side of the road was for your competitor. In horse collecting, the less common white horses counted double. But when your side of the road passed a cemetery, all your collected horses had to be buried. Not frequent travelers, we never remembered quite where the cemeteries were located; they just appeared around a bend in the road and too often the leading sum of horses vanished.

In those days, travel was slowed by the narrow, galloping highways, paved, but only two lanes. Near the farm, some secondary roads were paved with red bricks. We were told that the bricks were made by the men in prison; very impressive. The main roads meant that a parade of cars could form behind a burdened truck or ambling hay wagon. Eventually, passing a vehicle was an adventure for all because of highway turns and hills.

There were new things for city kids to see along the way. Farmers with roadside barns gained a free paint job by letting Mail Pouch use the end or side of the barn as a billboard. Black background, yellow letters proclaimed a product unknown us: Chew Mail Pouch Tobacco. Although the barns varied in size and shape, the message was always the same and so were the colors and the lettering. "Treat Yourself to the Best."

Recent gasoline stations were often just an added service of another business, a general store or machine shop. By the 1930s, blacksmiths had all but disappeared from the main roads and were replaced by car repair garages.

The gasoline pumps, which had to be hand cranked, featured tall glass domes displaying the red gasoline. As the car was filling, the gasoline sloshed around in the glass and slowly lowered to a mark showing how many gallons had been filled, at 18 cents a gallon. Only full service. Wash the windows, check tires, look under the hood, chat with the driver and passengers. Not so friendly were the rest rooms, more for the convenience of the grease monkeys than for the public. In a few more years, Clean Rest Rooms signs would urge travelers to stop and buy gas – after women passengers would first make an inspection of the clean-enough facilities for the family use.

Fantasy marked some independent gas stations as well as the newest rural eating places catering to increasing summer traffic. One

station featured a single-engine "crashed" airplane with its nose smashed into the garage roof. A real eye catcher. Others had older horseless carriages or buggies on their roofs. Refreshment stands sometimes clearly represented their names. The Bulldog stand was a building sculptured like a giant dog sitting beside the road. Its open mouth was the outdoor sales counter serving up candy bars, hot dogs, hamburgers and the latest soft drinks. The Weiner Dog stand was shaped like its name and featured hot dog sandwiches. The Lighthouse was tall and narrow with a revolving light, but had the same menu – no fish were served in those days of pioneer refrigeration.

Drive-in movie screens and their parking lots were daytime-empty as we dashed by. The favorite roadside attraction for us kids was the series of humorous shaving cream signs. Each spring they would pop up in another location; six small red horizontal signs – each a little bigger than a rural mailbox – at the edge of the road. Each was carefully spaced one after the other so they could be read by a car speeding by at 45 miles-an-hour. Series of verses with white letters always ended with the last sign in fancy script *Burma Shave* logo. Kids don't use Burma Shave so we only wondered why it came from so far across the ocean to Ohio. The rhymes were often amusing and mostly sent in by passers-by, we learned years later. We always read them aloud, demonstrating our reading skills and rushing ahead to include the next sign in the series sooner than could anyone else.

Popular verses included:

WITHIN THIS VALE	LISTEN BIRDS	PAST
OF TOIL	THESE SIGNS	SCHOOLHOUSES
AND SIN	COST MONEY	TAKE IT SLOW
YOUR HEAD GROWS BALD	SO ROOST AWHILE	LET THE LITTLE
BUT NOT YOUR CHIN	BUT DON'T GET FUNNY	SHAVERS GROW
Burma Shave	*Burma Shave*	*Burma Shave*

As an extra treat we detoured a bit in order to ride on the Car Roller Coaster. The roads themselves seemed hilly enough – our car swooping downhill to gain speed to make it to the top of the next hill without shifting gears. This special type of roller coaster was a series of timber-constructed hills covered in planks not unlike what the earli-

est plank roads must have been. For 50 cents, a car could drive once over the several hills. It was like a tiny amusement park roller coaster and it was designed so that what the hills lacked in height they made up for in stomach-dropping gasps. It was fun. I didn't think that our old Buick could do it, but it did. That special treat ended, we were on our way again.

After a few games, some lazy surveillance of the rural landscape, a few cookies, and one argument, more than two hours later we were well beyond the little Airfield and turning in to the narrow dirt road by the creek. No name or number, you just had to know where it was off the Savannah Road. The dust sprang from the arched ribbon of small stones thrown to the center of the road that clattered against the car bottom. At summer's end tall stalks of ripening corn crowded roadside fields so that the rural roads seemed like hallways with green wallpaper and a blue ceiling. We all looked ahead to see if another plume of dust might rise above the very narrow road. None. Even so, we honked just before the hairpin curve. Caution! A tractor or a horse drawn hay wagon quietly ambling along was always a possibility.

Then soon it was up Granddaddy's lane toward the farmhouse. At

first, only the roof peeked over the sloping field, then the white Dutch colonial house with its cheerful red trim around windows and doors. House on the left, three big trees, the lane, and the great barn and outbuildings on the right. Cats scattered as we pulled up next to the other cars. We kids piled out, grabbed a small take-this-with-you from Mother, and ran toward the kitchen door. Overhead, the giant fir trees in the front yard stirred and moaned in the breeze competing with the clucking chickens in their own yard next to the kitchen. The farm at last!

In the kitchen, the friendly wood-burning black iron stove bristled with steaming pots filling the house with a medley of scents all mingled together. "Ho! Del, they're here," Grandmother would call out. And Del, Granddaddy, would emerge from the back bedroom in his overalls stepping carefully – as if to avoid uneven ground. He always seemed more at home outside doing his many farm chores. Grandmother, the adults called her Emma, was rolling out thick noodles and cutting them carefully. It would be another feast, for sure. After the kisses, we checked the big ceramic cookie jar and sniffed its rich sugar cookies piled high inside – made with a magic touch of nutmeg – as uncles and aunt ambled in from the living room shrieking their welcomes with outstretched arms. But no other children.

"The girls and Bill are on their way back from the woods by now,"

Aunt Fern would assure us. Bill was our newest cousin and lived right on the farm. The girls, Joan and Margaret, also cousins, were from a town 15 miles away. "You boys fill the water glasses," Mother ordered before we could bolt outside. A parade of hot dishes and platters followed the already-set table, silverware, the special cut-glass goblets catching the sunlight and sending magical colors all around the room. The napkins were positioned just so along with huge flowers, colorful and grand center stage on the long table completed the setting. And soon all was readied for the groaning board.

Farm dinners were noon-time major meals, orchestrations of country ham, chicken, sweet and Irish potatoes, noodles, several vegetables, some mysterious homemade canned concoctions from the cellar, relishes and pickled things. Or there were greens salads, molded Jell-O's, celery & carrot sticks served in their special dish, and sometimes oysters – that once-a-year exotic treat for in-landers. Hot rolls and butter with, "Have another helping. You kids don't eat enough to keep a bird alive." Finally came the pies: apple, mincemeat with real shredded roast beef, cherry, berry, or lemon meringue, and even a spring-time pumpkin pie occasionally. No ice cream. That was for later.

After dinner and the reports requested by the adults about our schoolwork, we kids would dart to the barn: the horses, the cow stable, the hayloft, the wheat bin, the rusty corn sheller, and the milk house. Our one self-appointed task was to check the oats bin by the horse stalls and let down more oats through the chute if the feed bin was not full. The simple mechanics of a board shoved into the square wooden chute controlled the flow: board in = off; board pulled out = oats would flow down from the large storage bin above the ceiling. Then back into the house for the next event.

At Easter Time

Our family often went to the farm at Easter. With winter snows definitely gone, a trip through the countryside was a special treat. The smell of fresh-plowed earth and the thin veil of yellow-green leaflets on the trees gave hope for warm weather and the coming end of the school year. Easter had its special treats including the Easter egg hunt. Grandmother had colored eggs – always clear colors: red, yellow, blue or green, without any new-fangled store transfers. Sometimes a special mottled texture was made by wrapping a piece of netting around the egg about to be dipped into a cereal bowl filled with liquid dye..

One bowl for each color. The dye was bought in packets of dry powder. When emptied into a bowl of boiling water, the pale powder magically dissolved into brilliant liquid dye! Around the farm-house, the decorated eggs just appeared (from the Easter bunny) when we were tots, but dyeing our own Easter eggs became fun for us as we got older.

Easter morning always started the same way. Armed with baskets nested with green cellophane grass we frantically searched the house first for the chocolate rabbits that we knew had been hidden at the last minute, and then we stormed outside to a lilac bush in a near corner of the chicken yard. There, in a pile of rocks collected from the fields while plowing, we found colored eggs and more goodies hidden for us. The parents took a few photographs, we ate a few jelly beans, missed a few others, and the Easter egg hunt was over for another year.

Indoor, chocolate rabbits were reluctantly shared with the adults, but only after the ears were chomped off. We did not dare show our chocolate bunnies to Uncle Frank because he would always bite the ears off! (Ears are the best part.) Some were hollow, some were solid, and in those days they all melted rapidly on excited young fingers. "Don't touch anything!" kept us frozen until the hands, face, neck and occasionally a stray knee were wiped clean before we made a final sprint outside, the kitchen door squeaking and banging better than our city door ever could. A ring of the distant dinner bell would fetch us back to the house in a hurry to have the noon meal. Easter was a time for ham; ham that had been cured and smoked in the smoke house just yards outside the dining room windows. Springtime seemed to encourage fancy salads with cherries and marshmallows, candied sweet potatoes, and layered cakes with cream fillings. The table decoration celebrated Spring and Easter with more eggs and bunnies. A farm addition was marshmallow candy chicks, too.

After the meal, the grownups snoozed. They wandered off to all parts of the house in easy chairs, on sofas and the comfortable porch glider. Our dad was often the only adult awake. "I don't know why this family gets together – everyone just sleeps." Heavy holiday meals lured the adults to take some well earned relaxation. The dishes could wait and be washed later. We kids skipped naps and had urgent exploring to do outside.

When we returned, sandwiches and milk appeared with the delayed ice cream as the spring air suddenly cooled. The host aunt and uncle had been gathering stored produce, an "extra" ham or chicken, portions of our favorite pie to save the city folks from store-bought food. During the 1930s Great Depression, farm folk worried about city relatives surviving without large vegetable gardens. The three-times farewells were said as the car was loaded and then as twilight faded into darkness we drove away – back to the city, kids dozing off to the soothing hum of the highway.

Another happy one-day visit to the farm had ended.

Contrasts

The farm almost seemed like a different world to us in spite of the friendly people who were explained to us as being our relatives. Unlike some families in the city, we had no relatives nearby. The farm folk were our nearest relatives. Grandmother, Granddaddy, Uncle Frank and later Aunt Dorothy on the farm; Uncle Curt and Aunt Fern from nearby we knew fairly well and we knew that our mother, Blanche, had been a farm girl and was the sister of Curt and Frank. But other relatives were only part of adult conversation – a babble of names quite meaningless to me until one of the names would arrive in person and become real.

"Aunt Bea" was such a one quite familiar to my cousins, but seen only a few times by our family. She lived in town close to my cousins not too far from the farm, was a jolly person, and an excellent cook. In her back yard was a wonderful grape arbor. I had never seen one, a structure that arched over the walk at one side of the yard and supported the tangled vines, leaves, and clusters of forming grapes. Walking into the arbor, the flat sunlight of afternoon became a lively dance of sunny spots and dappled shadows; a delightful tunnel playhouse unlike any other.

In the farm country, our relatives enjoyed life much as we did in the city, but there were sharp differences, too. At home, we seldom saw a horse, never a cow, sheep or pig, but the cats and dogs seemed similar.

Differences in common speech were more evident. A paper bag at the farm was called a poke, and we were asked to fetch it. Their down-country accent was only slightly different from our city talk only sixty miles north. "Do you mind the time we went to town?" The

word mind could either mean remember or it could mean watch. "Mind your step so you don't cut your foot!" Cut always meant to step in the fresh manure pile of a cow or a horse.

There was one word that startled us kids. Our car went into the garage at night (ga - raw-ze). Granddaddy called it the gare-awge. This seemed quite peculiar to me. Years later, I learned that his pronunciation was a leftover of Colonial English that had migrated west from Appalachia more than a century earlier.

And there were other contrasts. Space was the most obvious one. In the city, we lived in an average three-bedroom, one-bathroom house built twenty years before on a small lot. Our tree lawn held one Norway maple at curbside, our back yard another, where wire fences were bordered with low bushes and flowers while pink and white hollyhocks soldiered by the side of our single car garage. The back yard was just big enough to play Indians, hold a kids' circus, and mow it with a hand reel mower while supper was being prepared. Neighborhood games were played in the brick street out front after supper beneath sheltering trees and a lone street light. In those days fewer families had an automobile, and never more than one. Many people gave up driving all winter; the car was put on blocks, the flattening tires removed. City trolley cars sufficed.

Our street in summer rarely saw a car after supper. People stayed home. So our games in the street were safe. We played Kick the Can. An empty tin can was booted and a victim's name called out to be "It." "It" had to retrieve the can and try to start catching the others busily hiding. When "It" sighted someone, their name and location were called out with one foot on the "home" can to officially catch them. Prisoners could be freed by someone leaping out of the darkness and kicking the can again. As parents called kids home, the end came as "It" called, "Awley, Awley, in free!"

Another game was Tap the Ice Box. Early refrigeration depended on an insulated cabinet with 25 lb. blocks of ice at the top. Ice was delivered to each house, the homeowner putting a card in the window showing the amount ordered. Kids chased the horse-drawn ice wagon and stole small chunks of ice from the wagon while the iceman, with a leather pad on his shoulder to hold the ice, made the next delivery.

Tap the Ice Box was another variation of Hide and Seek. While facing a tree with eyes closed, your back was the ice box. It was tapped by an unknown finger. The "ice box" tried to guess its owner to start the game.

We never thought that time after dinner for games was long enough. Our dad seemed to whistle us home earlier than any other kids. Sometimes we were told, "You come inside when the street light goes on," and somehow that always seemed to be later than Dad's whistle.

Compared to narrow city streets, the farm seemed to be mostly space. The farm buildings sat snugly in the middle of a quarter section, 160 acres, or ¼ of a square mile. Fields surrounded the cluster of house, barn, shed, barnyard, milk house, garage, pig sty, corn crib, chicken yard and hen house. A lane between the house and barn led out to the world of neighbors, town, Post Office, church, barber shop, and the Farm Bureau. Trees were confined to the house lawn and the distant woods. One lone tree stood in the center of one pasture, surrounded by shaded cows. The wind-swept waves of green fields reminded us of Lake Erie's restless waters. As we looked out, the fields blended with neighbors' fields separated only by the dashes of visible dirt road beside the steady march of wooden utility poles loping across the landscape.

All that sky! Suburban dwellers look ahead, or down, or up to a canopy of trees. Our home city was once known as "The Forest City" so not much sky. The skyscapes of the countryside were always present, not the spectacular sunsets over lake or ocean, nor the pulsating skies of mountain country, just plenty of open sky all day. Sometimes it was clear, hot, blue. Other times, great piles of cumulus clouds seemed to nod down toward us. When it did rain, somehow Granddaddy knew that, "It won't be clear until there is enough blue sky to make a Dutchman a pair of britches."

Sunsets were mellow and calm with a distant moo or bark accenting the blanketing haze. Small gleaming lights came from fellow farmhouses and barns as chores for the day ended everywhere with the faint clank of a metal pail. Stars were close and hung on threads (not like those city ones, faint and fuzzy). So many stars that the Big Dipper barely emerged from the confusion of glitter. Quietly lying on the ground face up, we could take it all in and feel the earth itself rotate until called indoors. The smell of the fields, plowed or green, made up for the uneasy quiet of night. We always slept well enough after busy days, but some city adults are startled and made sleepless by the unfamiliar silence of the countryside night.

In contrast, dawn brought a rush of sounds: the earliest birds, then roosters and eventually all of the animals greeting another day. Early cooking, early chores before sunup make demands everywhere on farmers and their wives. We knew that some tasks in the city were done in the dead of night, but they never touched us. The farm activities did. No matter what time we got up, it seemed that the day had been in high gear long before we came down to breakfast. We smelled the cooking, and we knew the men had already worked a couple of hours out in the barn. As we came downstairs, they were entering the kitchen for a second coffee after their earlier full breakfast. This meant breakfasts quite different from our off-to-school morning meals. We ate enough at home, but not so many things all in one meal. Farm style included bacon and eggs, and oatmeal, and pancakes or potatoes, even the occasional piece of pie as well as juice, milk and coffee. Then, a brief chat with kids and women and a discussion of the day's work to be done before the men headed outdoors again.

All work happened in open view on the farm. At home, we knew Dad worked – we visited his office at City Hall, saw his desk and chair, his drafting table, but had no details of what he really did all day, just "engineering". On the farm, we could see the horses hitched to the wagon, the stone boat, the cultipacker, the seed drill, the plow. We saw the last season field stubble being turned over, row after row, until the blanket of old tan and green became new brown and black; flat field became wave after wave of fresh plowed earth. Work progressed and everyone could see it happening hour by hour. Only the secret of growth lay hidden underground out of sight.

One other indoor contrast was in the farmhouse, the bathroom. Our small, city bathroom had everything we needed and sported a wainscot of subtly painted imitation marble. The bathroom at the farm had been indoors for many years. A converted bedroom, it seemed huge to us. There was even a bathroom back porch sitting above the woodshed and overlooking the chicken yard. A large side window framed two giant fir trees with a glimpse of the barn beyond. There were wide spaces between the fixtures, and taking a bath seemed especially strange in such a big room. It was like bathing in a public space, drafty and open for view – not like at home, snug and cozy. And the water was different. The soft rain water from the cistern required much less soap than we expected. Drinking and cooking water came from the deep well and was "harder" water with minerals.

A multitude of differences made the farm experience unique, whether it was for a one-day visit, or for our summer stay of several weeks. And, these differences were what made going to the farm so much fun; a new comfortable world with activities in contrast to our life in the city.

The Farmhouse

Our sister Barbara began her farm experience before my brother and I were born. She was the first grandchild. She knew the earlier farmhouse with its L-shaped cobblestone porch outside the front parlor. It wrapped around the side of the house to the kitchen door.

Cemented within the front stonework, an Indian tomahawk survives. That house was a typical gracious, comfortable farm residence, but no indoor plumbing or electricity. Some rooms served special purposes, now all but forgotten.

The fancy parlor followed the pattern of the last hundred years being reserved for special occasions and after church on Sundays. When a visit from the minister was expected the parlor was readied. The hall sliding doors were opened, the room aired, shades raised, furniture dusted, and the straw-filled horse hair sofa checked for mice! The minister's visit required our sister to reluctantly put on shoes and a clean dress. She was also warned to not say anything except, "How do you do?" With the arrival of the honored guest, Barbara sat quietly next to Grandmother and silently tried to unravel the tapestry of talk about local friends, neighbors and church. The visit concluded with everyone kneeling in prayer followed by light refreshments. Barbara was relieved it was all over, wondering what all the fuss was about, and returned to her bare-foot condition.

These old houses were subject to strange events. One day, just before mealtime, an ominous crackling sound alerted Grandmother. She quickly gathered everyone in sight. They dashed into the dining room and grabbed as much glass, china, silver and small furniture as they could while the loud crackling continued. Suddenly, the whole ceiling peeled away thundering to the floor in a huge cloud of plaster dust. The shrunken wooden lath had released the weight of the antique plaster. The ceiling was replaced and most of the furnishings rescued.

Sadly, the house burned one winter in 1926. It was a total loss by the time firemen arrived from the neighboring town of Sullivan. Some furniture had been hauled out in time including bedroom pieces tossed out the windows into the snow. The exposed root cellar of the burned house yielded burnt, and lower down in the bin, well-baked potatoes. Also, cooked carrots and onions in their bins. The home canned goods mostly survived, but some glass jars had exploded while others cracked and their contents spoiled. A shed was hastily put up by the neighbors and the surviving wood stove moved in. Life continued cabin-style during the months the new house was being constructed. Years later, that temporary shed was rebuilt to be the garage.

Our dad (to others, Ted) contributed some house plan ideas, and the new house incorporated part of the surviving cobblestone porch, plus later, new indoor plumbing – a special city feature and electricity. The new house had a living room (no parlor) and a woodshed attached to the kitchen. Eventually, the short pump in the kitchen was replaced by plumbed faucets, but still used the well water. The house was built on the old foundation with the surviving root cellar. The propped-up ancient cherry tree in the front yard gave up and was replaced with fir trees that quickly grew to a great height. These were the trees and the house that all of us young kids knew.

Remnants of an earlier orchard survived along with two cisterns behind the house. The underground cisterns collected rain water from the roof for washing uses. And there was the old unused out-house. Its elegant feature was two adult holes and a smaller hole po-

sitioned closer to the floor for children. Flies, the smell, the close quarters were common to both. The cesspool was only briefly glimpsed far down the shadowy shaft below the planks that served as seats. Within easy reach was the roll of toilet paper and can of lime to accelerate sewage treatment. In the new house, a quick flush and a septic tank did it all. This new house featured a recent innovation: a first floor powder room next to a back bedroom. This combination was to serve both aging grandparents in their declining years.

We loved the house over the years partly because it was in con-trast to our own city home. We never had a dirt floor root cellar with filled bins; only a basement with a concrete floor and laundry wash-ing tubs plus clothes lines draped with wet sheets row on row.

The farmhouse attic held special treasures for us. Rainy days found us up under the eaves exploring the retired items, some long forgotten by the adults. Wicker baby carriages, large dolls, a rocking horse leaking straw, arched-top mysterious black leather locked trunks with brass studs, and the grand prize, a hand-cranked Victrola. Its trademark label inside the lid was the patient dog carefully listening to His Master's Voice.

The gleaming mahogany cabinet with its sensuous curves held some very early phonograph records. Unlike ours, they were extra thick and a few were recorded only on one side. Opera stars' muffled arias hissed when the machine was cranked up and the silvery arm with the triangular cactus needle was gently placed in a quickly-revolving record groove – 78 quick revolutions per minute. We felt as if Thos. Edison himself were there listening with us. Soon, the music shifted key and slowed down urging us to hand crank the machine up again to full speed.

Sixty years later, Cousin Bill and his wife June love the same house very much – their home. The woodshed is part of a totally redone electric kitchen, the root cellar a rebuilt, furnished family room, the back bedroom transformed into a solid cherry wood paneled law library, and the finished attic is a cozy bedroom hideaway for their son. Lawyers don't farm, but neighboring Amish reap crops from the still fertile fields. The farm looks very fresh and happy, the fields are productive and the house, an up-to-date lively home serves new generations.

The Kitchen

The kitchen in the city house stayed the same year-round – stove, sink, refrigerator, cabinets. The farmhouse kitchen underwent seasonal changes. In summer, the cooking activities were protected from flying insects by spirals of sticky fly paper suspended from the ceiling plus a screen door that let in breezes and kept out most of the flies clustered on the screen outside, hoping to buzz in. The kitchen, large enough for all the usual things plus a generous eating area, even had an attached step-down woodshed. The kitchen was the preferred entry into the house; only strangers came to the front door.

In the winter, central to the kitchen's purpose was a big cast-iron wood stove. It featured six stove plates as access to the fire box below, next to an ample oven. Unlike our gas stove, the whole iron surface of this stove was hot, ready to accept many pots and pans filled with delicious concoctions. There was even a well for hot water on the side and an ornately supported back shelf above for storing small pans, utensils, and metal canisters of flour, sugar and salt. Proper sticks of wood for the heat desired were selected from the handy woodshed. Each different hardwood produced its own amount of heat. While there was a thermometer on the oven, Grandmother still relied on the brief hand-into-the-oven method of determining proper heat, a skill learned in earlier days. Sculptured scrolls, bold decorations in those days, gave this utilitarian black box some unexpected elegance.

Special were the fancy oven handles and the handle of the utensil to pry up the hot iron stove lids – polished thick wire coiled around the iron rod core was intended to keep the handles cooler. Still, a hot pad offered insurance against burned hands from the hot-everywhere stove.

The mixed aromas of each meal varied from eggy to spicy to sour as the menu changed meal to meal, day to day. "Something smells good," accompanied anyone who entered the kitchen near meal time.

One late winter visit, I decided to put the sugar maple tree in the front field to the test. Could that clear watery juice actually turn into bronze maple syrup? We had heard so much of the sugaring off in times past. Sugar keelers (wooden pails) and short spouts were attached to the trees at the last snowfall and received, drip by drip, the precious sugary sap as it rose inside the tree. Gathering sap from keeler after keeler into barrels supplied the large metal trough in the sugar shed where the liquid was slowly boiled down and down over a wood fire until it thickened. A favorite treat for children then was to pour some thickened sap onto the fresh snow where it instantly cooled into wiggles of maple candy. Slow cooking resulted in rich maple syrup, not the diluted type sold today in stores.

In the morning, I went confidently out, drilled and plugged the lone sugar maple tree, hung a small tin pail and waited. And waited. Going back hours later there was maple sap, sure enough! The small pail with a little sap in the bottom went to the kitchen where it was carefully poured into a small shallow pan on the back of the stove to be transformed into maple syrup. I could hardly wait. The vision of pancakes smothered in butter and dripping with my very own maple syrup filled my head. But, it was not to be. Sometime in the late afternoon, the pan was emptied by someone thinking it was only a bit of water and taking up stove space needed for vegetables. Such is life. What I did not realize was that my meager pan of sap would have only made one lick of maple syrup. It takes gallons of sap boiled down to produce the super market jars of maple syrup.

The kitchen was the scene of dedicated activity. One kitchen cupboard had a slide-out-shelf to increase working space. Grandmother, sitting on a stool, would place a few handfuls of flour on this shelf, some butter, a few eggs plus other vague amounts of other ingredients, combine them in a ceramic bowl with a glazed wide blue stripe around it, roll the mixture out and then cut slices that soon became thick egg noodles to be eaten with roast or stewed chicken.

12 cups white sugar
1 cup margarine
1 large egg
1 cup buttermilk
1 tsp vanilla
1 tsp baking soda
1 tsp baking powder
3 cups flour
2 tsp nutmeg
Cream margarine & sugar.
Add beaten egg, buttermilk,
and vanilla.
Measure flour before sifting.
Add soda, baking powder and nutmeg.
Drop from spoon onto cookie sheet
and top each with ¼ tsp sugar.
Bake in preheated oven for 15 mins
to 17 mins at 350 degrees.

There were dumplings some-times as well, and the famous Yorkshire pudding with beef. Leg o' lamb required real mint sauce made fresh from the garden. No commercial jelly here. The cooking took lots of time, but there was a patient expectancy about it that modern speedy cooking

misses. Through long experience, Grandmother learned that, "It takes less food to feed three men who say they are hungry than one man who insists that he isn't!"

Grandmother was always our favorite chef because she was the creator of the famous sugar cookies we considered the trademark for the farm. The large cookie jar was always filled for our arrival with big, round, tan cookies sprinkled with white sugar and flavored with a pinch of nutmeg – her secret ingredient. Those cookies dunked in milk were our favorite snack or dessert.

The kitchen table was the center for the breakfast shifts and we children were often the last to get up and last to eat. Often, with the milking done, the farm hands would join our table for a second cup of coffee listening to the brief farm reports on the radio – prices for grain, cattle, pigs, etc and the all- important weather forecast. Then, easy conversation often shared some special farm event with us. New piglets, a sick cow, new kittens, a scheduled trip to town or to a nearby farm. "Can we go?" meaning any youngsters around? "Sure, if your mother says so, and you won't scare the neighbors."

The kitchen table, at least when we were visiting, never served weekend dinners. The dining room was used for that. Much more elegant and roomier than the kitchen, it featured not only fine furniture but a generous bay window with its window seat crowded with an assortment of African violets, hanging baskets and house plants unknown to us, but favored and admired by the adults. The plants received ample light and bloomed accordingly. This cheerful room setting promoted happy meals and an occasional trick.

One holiday, a spilled bottle of ink appeared on the fully set, white linen tablecloth. Horrors! Aunt Fern was startled and so was our hostess, Aunt Dorothy, until they realized it was only a realistic spill made of black shiny metal, not ink. The ink bottle spill had come from a novelty store where whoopee cushions and rubber spiders supplied other anxious moments. Our mother wasn't so sure it was funny and scolded us. "Now, Blanche, the children have to have their fun," Aunt Fern would defend.

The kitchen table served in the evenings as a game table for the boxed games stored in drawers below the dining room window seat. On rainy days, occasional games of exotic Parcheesi would have us all together. Later, Monopoly swept the country with its popularity. Simple card games like Fish and Old Maid entertained us when we were small. Even a noisy round of Slap Jack was included. Barbara and the adults favored solitaire or bridge, too complicated for Dick and me.

The kitchen clock was of the school house variety with its gentle tick-tock and polished brass pendulum peeking back and forth tirelessly behind the clear spot in the frosted glass below the clock face. Thin Roman numerals gave the face a twiggy look and challenged our use of Arabic numbers. The instant connection from farm to the outer world was a crank telephone inside an oak case hanging on the wall. A firm crank would ring up "central" – the operator at the phone company switchboard. The party being called plus the farm number, six, double oh, six green, would be necessary to make a call. Rural phones were never private lines and party lines always had several customers on one line, some of whom listened in on every call. Incoming calls to the farm were identified by the operator cranking two short rings from "central" which also was heard by everyone on that party line. Private lines came years later to the countryside.

The view out of the kitchen window was of the lane, fir trees, the garage, the barnyard and barn. Out of this window over the sink, the heart of farm activity could be observed and visitors coming up the lane could be previewed before their vehicles stopped. Regular visitors to the farm included the milk truck to pick up big cans with the daily output from the cows, the egg truck to pick up candled and sorted eggs in their crates, and the twice-weekly visit from the town's Nickel's Bakery to deliver bread, pastries and other packaged goodies.

Come summer, the winter cast iron stove was put to use as a cold shelf, and the smaller more modern propane gas stove was moved into the kitchen from being stored in the adjacent wood shed. Gas wells were on some farms, but no piped-in gas was available here. This cooler source for cooking did require that the store-bought propane gas cylinder at the side be pumped up before each use. This supplied the necessary pressure to keep the gas reaching the burners; a function that fell to the gas companies at our city home where piped in natural gas was the rule. The gas stove was cream colored enamel with green trim so it looked more modern and summer-like than the somber wood stove. Light weight with thin curved legs, it was a deer compared to the wood stove bear. Here, the cooking was restricted to burner locations but the resulting dishes were just as delicious.

The kitchen today has been renovated again. The woodshed has added windows and with a raised floor serves as an extension of the kitchen proper. Great cooking continues today with June, Cousin Bill's wife, keeping alive a long tradition of eating well.

Country Fun

Our sister Barbara, being older, was the first to enjoy the farm. Her uncles and Granddaddy sensed her tomboy adventurous spirit, and their love of the practical joke sometimes got the better of them – and Barbara. After all, we've all heard of overturned outhouses, sheep on roof tops, and other rural pranks.

Barbara could easily be urged to try and ride a pig. Also, to dunk her head into the horse's watering trough, flecked with insects and oats floating in it. "No! Try this other one," she would be told. The "other" one being the clean water in the milk house trough which was much colder than anything she had ever felt. Her dripping, startled face brought a huge response. Trying to ride a pig was a similar disaster. "Climb that tree," was a feat more easily accomplished as was sliding down the new haymow inside the barn.

A climb up the ladder to the top of the hay brought her near the inside peak of the barn's roof. The cross-shaped vents in the plank wall made perfect portholes for looking over the barn yard, the house, chicken yard and the whole countryside. Walking on the hay put funny springs in her feet. And she could hear everything better up there. When the dinner call came, followed by a ring of the bell, one big slide down the hay mow brought our tomboy sister to the barn floor and on her happy way to the table.

A bigger challenge was sliding down the worn-down straw stack in the animal yard. This looked easy after the inside haymow. "You can do it," by the men brought her carefully into the animal yard which was only wet in certain spots. The short stack was readily climbed, but triumph at the top quickly changed to disaster after the quick descent down the side. Barbara landed on her feet, but plowed down through the thin straw  covering the muck below – a rich mixture of straw, hay, manure and lots of rain water – well, some rain water. The resulting gooey, smelly mess was not appreciated by the women who cleaned her up and chided the men for goading a little girl into pure nonsense.

By the time my brother and I were farm visitors, the fun had tamed down quite a bit. One time my brother, Dick, had trouble putting on his galoshes. Hard as he would try, they were simply too small for even his young feet. They were his galoshes, he was sure. He finally discovered wadded newspapers forced into each toe. Granddaddy was laughing, "Now what kind of a feller would pull such a dirty trick like that?"

When we boys became early teenagers we were given country advice. Granddaddy would solemnly advise us, "To make those hairs on your upper lip grow into a real mustache – feed them. Each morning just rub some horse manure on them to make them grow fast!"

Our Uncle Curt, Joan's and Margaret's dad, was a salesman for a local mattress manufacturer. Although raised on the farm, he chose to leave for a city career. Full of fun, he always had a trick at the ready. One of them involved a pencil on a loop of string. The pencil had Balyeat Mattress Company stamped on it, of course. Anyone wearing a blouse or shirt with button holes on the front was a fair target. Coming up close, he would instantly attach the hidden pencil through a button hole. Clever, but annoying when everyone discovered that the string was suddenly far too short to remove the pencil. Struggle as we would, hours would go by with pencils dangling from shirt fronts before we finally figured out how to remove them without ripping our clothes. We always enjoyed Uncle Curt's antics, but were never sure when his next trick would seize us. He never lost his farm skills and would milk cows, pitch hay, feed stock, and curry horses to help out his brother, Uncle Frank, the principal farmer, as Granddaddy became less active.

Not all of the fun depended upon grownups. We kids had our own games. City games like Tap the Icebox or Kick the Can seemed out of place on the farm, but hide and seek variations were abundant. With different age kids, a simple game like that let everyone play. The smaller children could always hide in impossible places and usually were last to be caught.

There were the "I dare you" events, too. The barn offered many tempting locations. Beam walking – wide, but very dangerous. Lots of old machinery to be investigated and the barnyard wooden fence rails to be walked with much waving of arms for balance. We seldom saw neighboring children when the family gathered, but during longer solo visits sometimes a neighbor child was introduced.

One sunny day, a neighbor boy about my age came over and suggested we go fishing. "Where?" "In the stream, yonder." "OK." I had never fished even though I lived on a Great Lake. Two long bamboo poles were found in the shed. Fish lines and bobbins were attached to small bent pin hooks. Outfitted in my new costume of overalls and he in his well-worn overalls, we trudged down the lane toward the fishing grounds carrying our gear and a can of freshly caught worms. Beyond the country road ran a rivulet wiggling along under great willow trees and flowing under a classic concrete arch supporting the lane to the neighbor's farm. This is where the fish were – or were thought to be.

The tiny stream had plenty of life in it. There were tadpoles, tiny minnows, crayfish, water walkers, but nothing ever so grand as a sun fish. Exploring the banks, hopping over the narrow waters, skipping stones and trying to fish gave us a pleasant afternoon beneath the shady trees. As shadows lengthened, farm chores beckoned my new friend away. Back with my family, I knew better than to brag about the one that got away.

I heard that in early spring that same little stream swelled to a generous depth, but I only saw it in late summer. Farm kids can't play much; their chores are clock and season regulated, and their duties differ only a little from the tasks of their father. Any contact with neighboring kids, therefore, is limited.

Our happy times at the farm took varied forms; some quiet, others high jinks, but often related exclusively to the people at the farm or the special opportunities that the rural setting offered.

The Barn

The barn was the largest of all buildings on the farm, and the boldest. American barns along with their giant silos have been called the early cathedrals of this country. They rose up over the landscape even before cities built large stone church towers. The abundance of tall trees in this wilderness led to great barns of lumber where fodder, animals, and tools shared one large building. One whole tree could provide a thick beam to span the width of a barn, or become a long roof rafter to create a vast space without extra vertical supports. Enormous barns are common in this country, but less usual elsewhere.

Our barn was a favorite playground, rain or shine. It was the first vast space I had seen. The size of the upper floor with tall haylofts and grain storage bins was made larger by contrast with the entry floor reserved for animals. That ceiling was just above adult head height to retain warmth in winter. The unheated barn depended on animal heat to keep it cozy.

The barn was usually approached from the kitchen door of the house. A short concrete walk under the fir trees with its rope swing led to the large space at lane's end, the open farmyard. The yard was wide enough to let horses, wagons and machinery maneuver, especially during threshing season. Just in front of the barn to one side stood the milk house while the watering trough and pump were centered in front of the main doors. To the right was the entrance to the horse stalls and, next, the fenced-in animal yard with straw stack and wide swinging gate. Here is where the cows came and went each day. Their milking parlor was beyond the horse stalls, nearer the back of the barn. Facing the barnyard or the lane were the pig sty, corn crib, and garage. It all seemed logical and well planned.

The barn plan included elements evolved over many years in many barns. The low ceiling of the animal floor helped keep the horses, cows and pregnant sheep cozy in winter. The airy upper floor not only held tons of hay, but had ventilation to prevent fermenting gases from igniting, a constant threat to barns everywhere. Lightening rods along the roof ridge protected during summer electrical storms. Decorative cutouts in the gable ends assured fresh air, also birds, bats and barn owls. None of the uncles smoked, only our dad with his city cigars – but never anywhere near the barn.

A feature of most Midwest barns is the barn bank, an earth ramp leading up to the hayloft floor made as wide as the two sliding barn doors to the upper floor. This ramp could have a threshing machine go up it and still there was room at the side for a hay wagon and horses. This was necessary to have the barn filled with ample hay for winter animal food. The grain storage bins were tucked under the front hayloft for convenience. Hollow wooden shafts let down oats and wheat to smaller bins close to the animal stalls below. Other

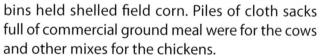

bins held shelled field corn. Piles of cloth sacks full of commercial ground meal were for the cows and other mixes for the chickens.

This great barn was built in the mid-1800s and, in spite of being unpainted, held up well due to the sturdy materials used by its builders. Only the wood shingle roof had been replaced. The corrugated sheet metal roof creaked and rattled in the wind producing angry, unfamiliar sounds as we played beneath. I had never heard a noisy roof before and wondered if it would ripple and fall. The whole barn exterior was a mellow weathered-wood grey, while inside floors, walls, rafters, were still almost tan. The milk house stood out in contrast with its white walls and red shingle roof, like the farmhouse.

There were clear regulations about milk houses and milking. One time, a milk inspector came by to announce a new regulation. The milking parlor had to be separated from the horse stalls during milking time. So a new sliding door was installed across the aisle way at the end of the horse stalls and dutifully closed during times when cows were in the barn. This meant that we had to be on time when milking began or miss the whole show. We never understood why the new door had to shut out even horse breath. That was grownup business. We continued to enjoy the milking activity, the one-legged stools and the many cats waiting for a well-aimed squirt of milk from a cow's teat.

Strangely, one of my favorite tasks was sometimes cleaning out the cow stalls while the cows were pastured. The dried dung and straw yielded easily to muck fork and shovel before the final sweep-down revealed the concrete floor. The area was ready for the next twice-daily milking. An hour of work resulted in the transformation from mess to neatness. Very satisfying.

A machine shed had been added behind the back of the barn to be close to the fields. Separate from the barn, it could only be entered downhill from the barn bank. Because it was largely out of sight, we thought little about it. But next to it was a beckoning attraction: a vintage Ford truck long retired from use. It had a strange steering wheel with a lever and notched, curved pieces at the center not unlike a sailor's sextant. This adjusted something. The truck seat was fully worn out with coil springs escaping. Oats and wheat chaff covered the bare floor boards, the rearview mirror was cracked and the  windshield missing. The small fuel tank was still under the seat, but long empty, its cap gone. I loved to play in the truck, steering 'round tortuous bends, climbing steep hills by making loud engine sounds, "Varoom-rooom-varoom!" My jostling the seat and noisy realism startled the gas tank inhabitants. Out they streamed, a squadron of yellow jacket hornets bent on removing the intruder from their truck. They plunged multiple stings into my shoulders and sent me bawling to the house with dozens of yellow jackets, now an angry black mass, in pursuit. As I burst through the kitchen door, the attackers retreated. My shirt off, and more whimpering, Grandmother inspected the damage. Calming me down, she applied thick slices of onion to the stung areas. Slowly, the pain subsided.

Later, Granddaddy and I set out to demolish the enemy. Armed only with a Flit gun loaded with insecticide, we crept up on the truck – I staying a bit behind. Powerful squirts of insect killer streamed into the narrow opening of the gas tank. "Get 'em, Granddaddy, get 'em!" I shouted. Any stray yellow jacket hornet that escaped staggered and fell to the ground. Mission accomplished, we walked hand-in-hand back to the house, I with relief, he with amusement. The truck was once again a safe playhouse.

The barn seemed to change more from season to season than did the farmhouse. Only Christmas decorations turned the house from home to celebration site once a year. The fresh Christmas tree just down from the woods quickly filled the house with its powerful pine fragrance. The tree decorations were quaint, some handmade, strings of popcorn, or ribbons and bows. Antique glass ornaments looked slightly worn missing bits of their silver decoration. The Christmas tree lights were similar to ours, but they had bubblers in them and ours didn't. Tales of wax candles on trees burning down houses recalled the childhood of our parents and our grandparents. They lived at Rose Hill a few miles away, known only to us through an antique photograph. The Victorian house was partly hidden by the austere lineup of bearded men and full-skirted women. The babe-in-arms was our own mother. So, Christmas was a time that briefly transformed the house and added a few unfamiliar holiday inhabitants.

Down in the barn the haymow was either full to the ceiling, or so low it wasn't much fun at all. Only the scampering mice were the same. The straw stack outside glowed like gold after threshing. It's great bulk challenged the rooftop of the barn. By the next mid-summer, it was a sad hump, a soiled mushroom, revealing how the cows and pigs had tried to chisel out a shelter to escape rain and snow. "Where did all the straw go,

did they eat it?" "Oh, no. We use the straw to bed down the animals in their stalls as well as in the outside yard. When the animals soil their straw, it has to be replaced with fresh."

After a few years of farm visits, it became clear to each of us that farming depended on a cycle of yearly events to survive. And the barn was the chief holder of all the fruits of the field dedicated to animal uses. Today, the barn stands, now freshly re-sided and painted white. The milk house, freshened before with a coat of white wash, has lost its distinction of solo white, and so it blends in with the whole barn. No milk cans rattle now; it is a cozy storeroom, cheerful and filled with light. The barn's bulk looms over the other buildings proudly declaring its heritage, now guarded by new farm dogs penned while cousin Bill, assisted by June, practices law at the county seat and state capital.

Milking Time

Our breakfast meal was often accompanied by the distant clanging of large milk cans in the milk house as the early morning chores ended. As the sun rose, the only thing we ever saw that early was the line of cows wandering back up the lane to pasture. Morning milking began when we were fast asleep. But evening milking time was the end-of-day entertainment that we counted on. A signal that it was show time found the herd of cows in the lane, down from the pasture and clustered before the closed gate. There were enough of them to require two milking sessions every morning and two every evening.

Although all the cows looked alike to us – black and white blotches on odd, boney, horned bodies – to our farmer relatives each cow was an individual, each with a distinct character and disposition. We never realized the social order of cows, with the Lead Cow head of the herd. Each cow knew her place in the herd and which stall was for her in the barn. The gate was opened; each cow went across the open barn yard, then in through the barn doorway next to the straw stack and to her proper place, one by one. The roomy neck stanchion collars were clanged shut when heads bent down. These kept the horned animals from backing up and disturbing the milking. The cows eagerly ate the   waiting shovelful of mash in the half-round concrete trough in front of them. This end of the operation was all heads and horns with agile rough tongues swirling up the last of supper, scattering stray morsels over the aisle in front. The feeding trough intrigued us. It was slick as marble and was licked clean twice a day. The horses' feed boxes were of crude wood with clinging bits of oats and stray corn kernels. We decided that horses were messy up front, and cows were amazingly messy behind. Even during the orderly milking hour, a cow down the line would arch its tail and plop loudly, and the floor drainage gutter was always well spotted afterwards.

In our early days, all of the milking was done by hand each cow's tail was first tied with twine to one leg to keep it from swatting the farmer. Seated beside each cow, milk pail between their knees, Granddaddy and Uncle Frank were balanced on their one-legged stools. Long ago the unknown inventor of these simple stools recognized that people have two legs, so a stool needs only to offer one leg to provide a firm tripod support. The music of the milk pulsing into the metal pails played a staccato composition in no particular key. We watched transfixed until a sudden squirt of warm milk arched over us as we jumped back in mock surprise.

With the first pails filled, a gang of local cats emerged and quickly scampered around an old cast-iron frying pan in one corner. They obviously had done this before. As the milk pail approached, a chorus of meows and up-turned faces suddenly changed to a pin wheel of backs. Then the milk descended into the pan and tails began to gently sway. The dozen cats became one multi-colored ring with only a glimpse of the white milk showing at the center. Every night, the farm cats – seldom seen during the day – added to their earned rodent diet with this treat during milking time.

Each milk pail after it filled was carried out of the barn and into the milk house with a few greedy cats following and begging. The milk house was a small white frame shed right in front of the main barn. Inside was a deep concrete trough filled with flowing piped-in well water. Several large shiny metal milk cans sat in the cold water. Within the neck of the open one, was a stainless steel strainer with a thick pad of soft paper. The fresh milk passed through this filter pad and strainer into the cooling can. The closed big milk cans sat in the water overnight until collected by the dairy company's big truck. The milk would be pasteurized and bottled by them in town. Each day, urban folks heard the milkman deliver the cream-topped glass quart bottles to their doorstep at dawn. Some houses, like ours, had a milk box built into the wall with little doors both outside and in as a convenience to the milkman and the housewife. In winter the cream would freeze and pop up the paper bottle lid displaying a little chimney of frozen cream until brought into a warm kitchen.

When twilight faded and crickets sang in the dark, a last pool of light surrounded the milk house as chores were finished. The cows lounged around the barnyard straw stack before settling down there where they spent the night. The cats darted in to lick the foam from the thrown out milk filters as the milk- house light flicked out. The stacked empty milking pails came up to the house to be scrubbed with hot soapy water in the kitchen sink. With the barn pole light out, the silhouette of the barn loomed against the darkening sky. Milking was ended for one of the necessary seven-hundred and thirty times each year.

The Lane

The dirt lane from farm to gravel county road was more than a driveway. It functioned more like a causeway to everything beyond the farm compound. Even telephone and electricity constantly came into the farm beside the lane. Only radio arrived without the poles along the lane. In a town or city, there were many varied connections to the rest of society and its services: sidewalks, gas, water, telephone, newspapers, electricity, sewers, garbage collection, police patrols, snow removal and street cleaning. Mail came either right to, or within, city houses. On the farm, even the mail was delivered down at lane's end. Self-sufficiency is the hallmark of rural life, yet farmers infrequently did rely on neighbors more than city apartment dwellers can imagine.

Yet, not everything useful was made on the farm itself. The obvious manufactured appliances, tools, machinery, furniture, as well as clothing, shoes, books, medicine, etc. had to be purchased in town.

Besides the milk and egg collectors, two regular services did come each week. First, was the daily mail. The roomy metal mailbox was required by the Postal Services Rural Free Delivery. It was mounted on a post at the foot of the lane. Pulled down to open on the road side, rounded top to shed snow and rain, name on near side, it featured a pivoting red metal flag on the opposite side. Red flag up

said, "Stop and pick up letters to go out even if we aren't receiving any mail." Red flag down put it out of sight of the Rural Free Delivery route man. From the farmhouse, the mail truck wasn't visible at the lane, but it could be glimpsed briefly across the corner of the field.

Running down to get the mail was always a chance to see a less familiar part of the farm. Young legs made the task easy. Sometimes, a small animal would dart across the lane. Other times, butterflies, or wildflowers like Blue Sailors (chicory) would delay us. Often, Tricksey, the fox terrier, would lead the way and dutifully not go into the road. In the quietness of the countryside, we could hear the hum of the electrical wires on the utility poles bordering the road. On a hot summer day, a quick, refreshing drink of cold water came from the pump halfway down the lane. It took several pumps of the big handle before a gush of cold water would arrive. After a drink, the pump handle had to be down or the pump would not work next time when stock or a team of horses had to be watered.

The other service came twice a week. The Bread Man drove up the lane to deliver loaves of bread and a variety of not-easily-duplicated groceries that everyone used. No point in bringing vegetables, fruits, or cream unless they were mushrooms, lemons, and whipping cream. What different farm households made or bought varied. This house baked rolls, noodles and pies, but less often, bread. Other farms never bought bread, but depended on other items that the Bread Man carried door to door. His Nickel's truck suddenly appeared and the whole side of the truck opened to display shelves with a variety of fresh and packaged items. Aunt Dorothy was the chief shopper with an occasional begging suggestion from us kids. Like most grocers, there were some items aimed at youngsters. This door-to-door service reinforced the completeness of the farm unit and infrequent contact with town. At our city home, trips to the store were frequent and necessary except for the ever popular annual bumper crop of back yard tomatoes.

The farm vegetable garden was placed at the edge of the closest fields and its location was rotated year to year. It was a lumpy texture of different greens and always provided plenty of variety and produce. The sweet corn and popcorn occupied the closest two rows next to the fence in a large corn field. Having it over there kept tall corn away from shading the shorter vegetables in this kitchen garden. Vegetables this close to the farmhouse ensured freshness. Uncle Frank would insist that the water be boiling in the pot before he would go outside to pick the sweet corn. "You know, the instant you pick the ear, the sugar in the corn will begin to change its taste, so the water should be boiling," he would say.

Some local farms specialized in truck farming to supply nearby towns and even Cleveland. A trip once to a nearby celery farm was startling to me because of the absolutely black dirt in which celery stalks thrived. The soil looked to me like coal dust or asphalt. The vast acreage of jet black was checkered with hundreds of orderly mounds, each topped with a bouquet of yellow green celery leaves, the stalks hidden from the sun within the mounds ensuring their whiteness for higher market prices. The orderliness and precision of the field made it seem more like manufacturing than agriculture.

Heavy rains changed dusty roads and lanes into slippery adventures for all motor vehicles. The great advantage of comfortable enclosed cars in bad weather did not offset the disastrous effect of spring rains on unpaved roads. One time, when our Uncle Curt arrived with his family, he was a victim of the violent spring rains. Turning into the farm lane, he bravely accelerated uphill toward the farmhouse. The soggy lane would have none of it. Sliding and swirling, he ended up in the ditch. Like many another "horseless carriage", the car had to be rescued by a team of horses and a stout rope. Cousin Joan wasn't worried about their car as much as "those poor horses working so hard to pull that big car uphill." Each summer, after the rains ended, the lane was oiled and scraped flat, free of ruts until fall.

Not everyone who came up the lane was welcomed. The hurried telephone message – easily listened to by any of the other six parties on the line – alerted the area to gypsies. Infrequently, roving gypsy families plied the countryside where community regulations were less restrictive than in towns. Their merchandise or services were not always needed and a watchful eye and ear always monitored their visits. A sudden pig squeal or flurry of chicken wings could mean that a free meal was being taken by the visitors.

In Depression times, men "coming through" looking for work were sometimes offered a night's lodging in the barn after quick evaluation by the kind, but wary, farm men. What city folks would never risk, farmers sometimes did. They were used to living with changeable crops, skittish animals and uncertain weather. Life was chancy. They had to have a large measure of reliance and trust in the Almighty to risk so much year after year coaxing the land into productivity.

One day, the lane brought a new dog to the farm after faithful Tricksey, old and feeble, died. The farm was only without a dog for a short time. Bounce, as he was named, arrived unannounced and un-tagged, a black and white sturdy dog of uncertain ancestry. Efforts to locate his owner yielded no information other than "the dog had been seen around." Bounce quickly adopted this farm as his farm. He was a more typical working dog and not as much of a family pet as was Tricksey. He showed little evidence of urban origins and was content to be with the other farm animals, the barn his comfortable home.

His specialty was herding a stray pig. All you had to do was shout "PIG" and Bounce would spring into action sniffing out the escaping swine and urging it back to the safety of the pig sty.

Today, with Bill and June at work in town, the only resident animals are stray cats and two guard dogs at the barn that hold forth until the Amish neighbor brings his team of horses up the lane to work the fields. Just for a few brief moments, things look much as they were.

Threshing Season

In the summer found us, one by one, on vacation at the farm for a week
or two. A seasonal excitement could be felt when the ripe fields shifted from pale green to deeper greens or to gold. Talk of when each field could be harvested occupied dinner conversations. Radio weather reports supplemented weather eyes scanning the western horizon. The oats and wheat fields yielded to the reapers cutting the grain and bundling the stalks into sheaves with twine, dropping them regularly across the field. The neighbor farmers shocked the oats sheaves so that each field was now occupied by an army of straw tents waiting in formation for hay wagon and threshing machine.

Bit by bit, evidence of the imminent threshing day occurred. First came the coal truck that deposited a small pyramid of coal by the barn bank. It was unusual to see a large truck in those days. Cars came and went, farm machinery and horses were sometimes on the roads, but seldom a big truck – they were city vehicles to us. The coal pile was a sure sign that threshing day was very soon.

The next sign was not outdoors, but in the kitchen. A flurry of activity all day produced a row of pies, tubs and crocks covered with dampened cloth, a bushel of potatoes from the root cellar. And a crowded stove top. The funeral director in his limousine delivered folding wooden chairs with a stenciled label Gilbert Funeral Home on each back and stacked them on the front porch. Heavy planks from the barn and saw horses from the shed combined to create a very long table in the shade of the fir trees in the front yard. This meant that the next day was the day.

At barely dawn, a noisy, unfamiliar steam tractor with two giant-studded steel wheels plodded up the lane and rested close to the barn bank and the coal pile. This was followed by the stream of assorted cars, teams of neighboring horses and hay wagons. Farmers greeted each other and scattered around the farmyard and barn busy with chores unknown to us. Shortly, a distant rumbling announced the arrival of the threshing machine. Over the brim of the roadside field there appeared a dinosaur-like head and neck bobbing slowly toward our lane. Suddenly it changed direction and swept slowly into the lane with freight-train intensity. The clattering increased as its dusty red bulk blotted out the garage and the shed on its way to the barn. The star had arrived. With obese difficulty it struggled up the barn bank, rattled over the upper floor of the barn and stuck its neck through the now open bay doors overlooking the straw stack. I never thought that two sides of the barn were mostly big doors, but now the barn looked like an open airplane hangar with the red thresher squatting over much of the upper barn floor.

At this season, the straw stack was low and scooped out all along its base by the animals constant rubbing. It was dirty and scraggy from the weather, manure, and rot.

Soon the work horses, hay wagons and farmers scattered out to several fields with organized determination. Clear skies encouraged success. The steam tractor by the coal pile and the thresher joined forces by way of a giant figure eight belt whose deliberate motion could be measured by the black steel fingers that joined its ends. As the belt loop traveled from steam tractor into the barn to the threshing machine and back, the black joint dutifully traced the journey each time. Watching for it to disappear into the barn and then reappear amused us. Coal was faithfully muscled into the fire box of the tractor to keep everything running. Big puffs of black smoke signaled each new shovelful making its mark.

As the horse-drawn wagons returned from the fields, they stomped up into the barn and their contents were fed to the voracious giant as it spewed bursts of golden straw onto the growing straw stack. We thought that this was the whole idea, not realizing that the grain filling up the feed bins was the major object of all this activity. The fields yielded their gifts and slowly changed appearance losing their temporary harvest sculptures to wagon after wagon. Bare stubbled ground is everywhere.

At mid-day the shrill whistle on the steam tractor blew and activity slowly waned. Farmers rolled up their sleeves and washed their pale forearms in the basins lined up for them on planks before sitting down under the fir trees. Lunch, or dinner as the farm knew it, was ready. The dinner bell by the kitchen door, a relic from a closed schoolhouse, formally pealed meal time.

A brief grace was offered by host Uncle Frank, and the feast began. Platters piled high with ham slices, bowls with fried chicken, mashed potatoes, ears of sweet corn that had been planted to ripen on cue (and picked minutes ago), cottage cheese, sweet potatoes, corn bread and relishes were passed around to each seat at the endless table. A spirit of tired conviviality prevailed. Some dishes passed by in a blur, vegetables and concoctions rejected by us children, but favored by the adults.

We were soon full, but the noon meal continued for the hardworking neighbors. After pie and coffee, the table suddenly emptied and the farmers streamed back to their work in the fields leaving compliments with the waiting farm wives whose preparations were always much appreciated. Now was the time for the women to sit, eat and talk. Then, the table was cleared and the kitchen organized for the massive cleanup. The wives welcomed the chance for more relaxed conversation with everyone now fed.

We lost interest after eating and resumed our children's games now that we had seen how it all worked. Near twilight, the whole procedure reversed itself. Gone were the fields of grain, but the straw stack glowed anew rising nearly as high as the barn roof. Bits of new straw were wind scattered over the yard and lane. The straw stack would settle a bit lower after the fall rains.

The tractor and threshing machine moved on to conquer other farms leaving behind only random chunks of coal. The army of farmers left in wagons and cars, the horse teams clomped down the lane and all was quiet again. Crickets chirped, a stray chicken voiced a protest, the dog barked, and darkness deepened in the woods as the kitchen lights came on.

Chickens and Eggs

The chicken was a highly visible resident of this farm. There were many more "laying hens" than other livestock. The chicken yard was just beyond the kitchen entrance of the house and much in evidence by sight and sound. The soothing murmur of chickens in their fenced yard and in their long houses continued all day punctuated by an occasional rooster crow.

Day after day the same murmur went on until suddenly the whole chicken population was noisily terrified. We had only to look up to see the cause; a chicken hawk slowly wheeling on an updraft. Although high in the sky, the chickens knew it could see them scurrying into the hen house and safety.

We welcomed the order to, "Go gather the eggs from the hen house. The baskets are in the woodshed by the back door. Remember to get every nesting box and don't be afraid to reach under a hen on her nest." We knew that was a challenge. My little brother was flopped once by an aggressive chicken determined to flatten him with repeated pecks and beating wings.

My older sister, who was five years bigger, went with us to supervise and to bolster our courage. A cautious approach to the hen house is necessary. Quiet foot steps. The door is opened slowly and we enter carefully midst a flurry of feathers, cackles, dust, straw, and a burst of manure smell. Standing silently for a few moments, things settled down a bit. Then the gathering begins. The nests are wooden boxes about a foot square lining the walls beneath continuous windows on each side of the long hen house. Down the center between the roof-supporting posts is one long wooden trough for feed, another for water. Chickens seemed to eat and drink frequently.

We creep down the right side. Some boxes have no eggs or chickens, other nests have several eggs, most only one. Some hens simply hop out of their nesting boxes and cluck away. Others try to hatch their eggs and resist the egg gathering. If they won't leave the nest, a hand has to reach into the straw under the chicken and feel for eggs. The determined hen gives up and staggers out of the nesting box.

We pick up each egg carefully and place it in our basket lined with soft newspapers. All the eggs are white as are all the chickens – white Leghorns. A few of the hens are comedians in their pink glasses. Chickens with glasses? Odd. Grandmother later explains that these are the aggressive ones who cannot see blood when wearing pink glasses.

Several chickens have to be urged from their nests, sometimes a warm egg or two under them. Other times no egg at all. Occasionally, a chicken is asleep on her nest. Barbara deals with that. Proud clucking down the line signals that another egg has been laid.

With our baskets heavy with eggs we quietly leave and are glad to be outside in the yard and allowed to talk again and walk normally. The gate in the chicken yard high fence is opened and then securely latched behind us. Eggs are delivered to the kitchen.

In the evening, the egg factory opens on the kitchen table. Each egg is candled. Not with a candle, as the name suggests, but with an electric light. Each egg, one by one, is held up to the light bulb revealing a blurry egg interior. Very rarely, an egg is rejected because it is not fresh or more rarely, even has evidence of a chick forming within.

Next, they are sorted by weight into three sizes: a few rejected small pullet eggs, from young hens, medium eggs, and large ones. The metal scale has a pointer that swings upward as each is weighed. If the egg comes within a certain marked zone, it is okay and ready for sorting and polishing. Medium and large eggs go into separate egg crates. Each egg is examined carefully. An extra long egg probably has two yolks inside.

Very rough surfaces are lightly sanded with a scrap of fine sandpaper to remove tiny bumps. These eggs have tough shells due to minerals in their special chicken feed. Then the polishing takes place. With a dampened cloth, every egg is rubbed to reveal a reflective surface; they look like white marble. Special racks cradle each egg and stacked crate after crate of eggs stand ready to be collected next morning. The "Egg Man" takes them to be put in cartons for the grocery stores.

Chicken sometimes was served roast or fried either at the noon dinner or evening supper. Aunt Dorothy did most of the cooking, while Grandmother fixed stewed chicken and dumplings and other specialties. On these days she needed an extra chicken. "You don't get enough flavor from only one chicken," she observed.

Killing Chickens

We never made much of a connection between the chicken yard and chicken served until we saw the chickens we would eat, caught and killed. Selected chickens – "Get a fat one for the dumplings" – were cornered and caught. Then, Uncle Frank carried them upside down by the feet while they gently murmured on their way to the chopping block by the garage. Anticipating the sudden chop steeled us for the inevitable. In the city, deliberate death of creatures was confined to mice and flies. Here, death and life were intermingled. We were startled by the axe chop and really shocked to see a headless chicken running around briefly. When Grandmother killed a chicken, she preferred the neck-wringing method.

None of us ever refused the chicken dinners, but we did recognize that our meals involved sacrifice. The hen house chickens kept on laying eggs and only a few were eaten by the family.

The flock was occasionally restocked with purchased pullets rather than allowing brood hens to raise their own. In spite of that, a hen would sometimes hide a nest in the yard and a family of fluffy baby chicks would parade suddenly around the yard led by proud mother hen; a pleasant addition to the always changing farm scene.

Horses

Dick and Tom were a team, a pair of white horses frequently seen working together. Distant flashes of white flicked across a distant field – separated from the rich earth and dark machinery. The horses seemed to be friends and in the barn would converse across their adjoining stalls and peek at each other though the openings between the stall boards. Their associate horse was Bob, a dark chestnut, slightly bigger horse. They all seemed huge to us, especially the hooves and their feathered fetlocks. When three horses were at the watering trough it felt as if there were several more. Stamping hooves clustered together. So many legs. We were warned to stand clear of the horses and we knew that they were heavy but agile, and could change direction quickly. We also heard of the occasional barn kitten that was accidently stepped on by a horse, and usually died. Our only contact with beasts at home was through the bars at the zoo, or the annual visit of the organ grinder with his nervous monkey begging for pennies. But here, a draft horse close up was another thing. To see one shimmy his skin while a flicking tail warded off insects made us realize that this beast was real and could do things that we could not.

Our earliest adventure was to get a horsey ride. Riding was reserved for tiny tots and done bareback as these horses were "work horses and not used to being ridden," Uncle Frank explained. Sitting tall without a saddle, we were higher than on Dad's shoulders. Our young legs were almost in splits to straddle the horse's broad back. When Tom put his head down to graze, half a horse disappeared and what was left seemed like a scary white slide. The horses' manes were long and bounced along in spite of our firm grip. The gait of the horse caused us to roll side to side and squeal as our uncle-guided journey continued around the farmyard witnessed by amused adults.

One of my favorite horse memories is the time Granddaddy hitched up the stone boat used to clear the field of dangerous rocks that could damage farm machinery. The stone boat was a sturdy wooden sled without sides, and heavy wooden runners. In pioneer days, sleds were used in summer as well as winter to haul materials across soggy ground unfit for wheels. A single-tree hitch to Dick provided our moving power. I was dismayed as where we would be, but Granddaddy stepped aboard the platform and I did also – not sure how this worked. With a "giddap" we were off, and the name boat seemed correct as grass raced under us like green ripples of water while the platform pitched and rolled over the ground. The handy adult pant leg provided my emergency support. When we entered the dirt lane toward the woods, the ride got rougher and nosier over the many ruts. At each field gate, we would stop, load on the few collected smooth rocks that had been thrown up by plowing, and then move along to the next field. Surrounded by rattling rocks, we would head back for the distant barn, our task finished.

The selected field stones were piled beyond the barn bank and supplied odd construction and repair jobs around the acreage. Most winters produced a good "crop" of rocks heaved up. Each spring, rocks in the fields would have to be removed – even on this good land.

When horse fly season came, the horses wore special gear, a sort of net-like blanket of thin leather strips that jiggled the big flies from the horses as they moved. When out of harness, Dick and Tom would stand head to tail and together their tails would flick flies in all directions. Bob, the chestnut horse, worked just as hard as Dick and Tom but seemed less of a personality to us. Eventually, as we grew up, the horses were retired and then disappeared, replaced first by two mules that we didn't understand or like, and then by the smelly gasoline tractor. But horses can still be seen on adjacent farms, thanks to recent Amish neighbors.

The Amish in Ohio, Indiana, Pennsylvania, and parts of Canada are often farmers who stick to their old ways and raise bumper crops with natural fertilizer, skillful land use, and many sons to do chores. Their farms are easily identified by not only horse, but no electric lines from road to house. Their preference for simple ways is a religious resistance to worldly, materialistic concerns that might lure them away from focusing on worshiping God. "

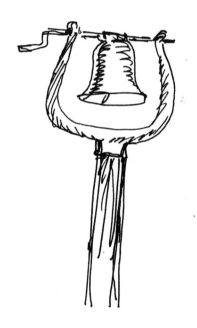

Pigs and Sheep

The abundance of animals scattered everywhere was the one most un-citylike aspect of the farm. I was a city boy with only gold fish for pets. Our mother did not like animals in the house. Her farm upbringing required animals to be in a barn. It was an era when city zoos were mostly steel cages with sad animals looking self-conscious. There was only a slight difference between the colorful circus wagon with pacing tiger and the black steel zoo cage with pacing tiger. To see animals loose out in the open air was a new delight to us. Frisky lambs, riotous pigs, or languid cows were right at home out-of-doors.

This farm had cows, but no steers – only a visiting bull whose job was to re-populate the dairy herd. There were times when the bull was unsuccessful in his mission. "The spirit is indeed willing, but the flesh is weak," Uncle Frank would say, carefully quoting the Matt.26:41 biblical passage. Milk was the cow's product sold, not beef. The meat producers were the pigs and the sheep.

Pigs were housed in a sty that opened to the animal yard with its centerpiece, the straw stack. The sty was a separate small shed near the main barn. Cows came and went from the shadow of the straw stack with their busy schedule of milking, pasturing and more milking. The pigs out-numbered the cows and were the main inhabitants of the yard. Their world was confined to sty and yard. Once in awhile, a pig would escape, announced by much squealing from the pig community. They never went far, they knew where the food trough was, and they knew Bounce, the farm dog, was on guard.

Do pigs eat like pigs? Yes. With two feet in the trough pushing each other aside amid such snorting nastiness that you'd think that they had not eaten for days! In addition to pig foods, they were the consumers of kitchen scraps – perfect food disposers. We would carry a tub of salad scraps, plate scrapings and who knows what, to the pigs. They could smell it coming and, leaving the shady comfort of the animal yard, would squeal into the sty and jockey for trough position. Dumping the scraps into the trough wasn't always easy for us small people. The board rails to keep the pigs in left only narrow spaces through which to shove the food. The pigs did not trust us. We tried to spread the morsels the whole length of the trough to feed all, but the pigs piled over each other wherever we dumped as we moved along the trough. Beady eyes pleaded with us while fluttering pig ears waved over noisy snouts. "Pigs is pigs." Other times, the pigs were fed their ears of field corn stored next to them in the corn crib. A percussion concerto, with the corn ears rattling and thumping against the wooden trough, was punctuated by crunching pig teeth.

After the frantic feeding, the pigs retired to the cool mud of the yard. Mud also protected them from flies, as they found favored spots around the shade of the straw stack and drifted into a piggy snooze.

A special event for us was the arrival of piglets – so cute, so small, so pink, so many. Could they ever grow into the monster sow that was their mother? All those piglets lined up for lunch, each at a "faucet." You could see why mama had to be so big and long! Babies of any kind are always an attraction, but baby pigs, pink and smooth, seem strangely akin to people.

At the other extreme was the occasional butchering of a pig for pork, hams and bacon. A metal tripod, wood fire, and giant iron kettle were the sinister tools to begin it all. We never watched the whole thing, but vaguely knew that it was happening. Grandmother stuffed cleaned intestines to make sausage – a sharp revelation to us – and we saw the hams taken to the smokehouse behind the farmhouse. A small hickory fire, kept going for days, cured the hams. The smell was delicious and helped us to forget how the hams got there.

Then there were the sheep, a flock of sheep. Few individuals there. Out in the far field they moved slowly in a group across the pasture. Later in the day, they disappeared over a low hill. We seldom saw them up close, but when we did their thick wool with its oily depth felt almost artificial, so unlike dog, cat, cow or horse hair. The sheep always seemed shy and sweet and surprised us with their big voices. The spring lambs were born in the barn, their spindly legs and long tails unlike their mother's. This was the only time we saw sheep close up, except when they left to go to market.

On that day, a mass of lumpy sheep flowed down the pasture lane and had to be herded across the open yard in front of the barn to the truck. The sheep sensed what were happening, all those strange waving arms and hats, the close fences. Finally, the last one was loaded up the ramp and off they went down the road to town, the truck bumping along in a swirl of dust. The far pasture is empty.

Into Town

"Going into Town" was always a pleasant change during an extended farm visit. We city folk felt more like ourselves in town, even though it was different from our city. Suddenly, there were sidewalks, parked cars, signs, and groups of shoppers just like home. An occasion for a trip to town was a haircut, church, clothes shopping, or the Farm Bureau.

The county seat was not small, but everyone seemed to know lots of people on the street. Our Uncle Frank was especially recognized because of his official status in the Farm Bureau. While he took care of business, Granddaddy and I would leave for the Barber Shop. Ahead was the familiar revolving pole with its red and white stripes. The Barber Shop was down a short flight of stone steps right off the sidewalk. Immediately inside was the giant sucker tree with its array of colorful round suckers, their wooden sticks thrust into holes in a 4" x 4" tree post. The suckers were always good, but not available until a haircut had been endured. In the city, haircuts were 50 cents at Fred and Bill's where Dad and I went. Here, they were only 25 cents, with a free sucker, too.

Barber shops were the same everywhere. The linoleum floor sprinkled with hair clumps, the big chairs, old magazines, the potted plants in the front window. The line-up of different aromatic bottles of Bay Rum, Witch Hazel and Wild Root hair cream suddenly made double by the wall of mirrors. Passing the boot black stand, spice shifted to the stronger scents of shoe polish and leather. To the click  and snip of scissors, and the all-male cast emptied chair after chair. Women went to Beauty Parlors. We went to the public mens' club – the Barber Shop. Man talk filled the air with largely farm concerns here. Lots of weather talk, crop prices talk, machinery talk, government policies talk – especially concerns about government regulations, plus the inevitable hospital news discussed – who is in, who just got out. No personal situation escapes notice in a small town. Hospital entries are even broadcast daily on local radio.

After the final snip, the warm shaving cream was brushed on the neck for the unfamiliar straight razor. Sharpened on the leather strop, it cautiously cut off the stray stubble around the ears and back of the neck. Holding very still was expected, obviously. A brisk rub with a fresh towel, the hair roughened and doused with fragrant tonic, hair plastered down damp, then carefully combed, and the neck swept clean with talcum powder completed the operation. The great striped billow of cloth was flicked off by tearing the paper neckband. The only act remaining was to pay the barber and then select the perfect sucker from the sweets tree waiting by the shop door.

Outside in the squinting-bright sun, the cloud of fragrant hair tonic followed us down the street. The slight dampness behind each ear slowly vanished as we passed the shop windows filled with dresses, shoes, perfumes, hardware and other un-farmlike merchandise. A special treat down the street was a stop at the Sanitary Dairy. Their extra-creamy ice cream was always rich; the cones piled high with favorite flavors. We met Uncle Frank near the car where he was discussing Farm Bureau business with a few other farmers who were in town. The big picnic event of the season by the Farm Bureau is an "Ox Roast" held before the annual County Fair.

A few days later found us all there. The County Fair would be a week later, but by that time I was back in school. Plenty of food, and good food, makes Farm Bureau picnics very popular. Everyone dresses up. (I didn't know that farmers owned suits and ties.) Print dresses and bobbing big hats identify where the feast is being set up from baskets of home made specialties. Cars and trucks of all vintages are lined up casually at the edge of the field. Rows of plank tables are dressed in multicolor tablecloths held down from the occasional breeze by bake bean pots, picnic baskets, and thermos jugs. On each table side is a line up of folding chairs, stools, and old kitchen chairs of every description and height. Seats for kids are readied with apple boxes to raise eager eaters to attack level.

"Where's the ox?" "Well, it really isn't an ox, but a whole side of tender beef." Standing in line, a paper plate with a big open bun on it, readies each of us for the encounter with the "ox" that is slowly rotating over a long charcoal fire. A sturdy server with his official chef's hat and white apron deftly slices off a slab of beef and slaps it on my plate– almost hitting the bun. Next come the many choices of things in bottles and jars to enhance the meat flavor followed by the main dishes both familiar and unfamiliar. Vegetables I had never seen before appeared in exotic sauces. "You must try some of Mrs. So-and-So's homemade specialty." Lots of urging, but I'm a picky eater, not like the appreciative farm hands ready for a third helping. Still, there is plenty to eat. While charcoal roast beef is the feature, there is the smell of fried chicken and wieners for little ones. Brought from home are vast quantities of potato salad, roasting ears, baked beans, multi-layered cakes, and enough lemonade to float a boat. Eating is the main event. The kids gobble down, escape to seek out each other and play wildly while the adults are left to hear the thanks-for-supporting-your-Farm Bureau speech followed by ap- plause and a brief sing-along led by a trio of high school girls.

The Ox Roast is put on by the Farm Bureau as its annual money maker. This one must be a success judging from the attendance. Lots of families are there with active youngsters who eventually wind down and get fussy. Everyone leaves by early evening. After all, the cows have been waiting.

Bill Arrives

For a long time, we were the only children at the farm. Uncle Frank married a bit later then some men and his bride Aunt Dorothy, a teacher from a small Pennsylvania city, was busy adjusting to unfamiliar farm life. But later, word came that a new baby had arrived on the farm, Bill.

Over the years, a parade of babies had been introduced to the fascinations of the farm; Barbara, Ed, Margaret, Joan, and Dick in our group, and now there was a farm-born child. It was clear to us that although younger, he knew much. Bill knew our familiar haunts, but also he really knew much about actual farming that escaped us.

What began as a wide range of ages eventually seemed to shrink. When Barbara was in college, Cousin Bill had just arrived. By the time Bill was a teenager, we were all on more equal footing. But at that time, with everyone's many activities, school and work, the sojourns to the farm were less frequent. As the years passed we were living our own lives in separate parts of America. Next, Bill too was away at college and afterwards off to law school.

Years later, he inherited the farm and wisely chose to keep it for his bride and new family although his law practice meant that others tended to the fields. Motor bikes replaced horses, television replaced thick phonograph records, yet the farm continued to be cherished and protected by VanTilburgs, conscious of its many enduring values. These values speak to and transform each generation that witnesses the power of the land, nature, hard work and the miracles of regeneration.

Fences

"Good fences make good neighbors," poet Robert Frost reminds us of the old saying. Fenced farms cover the Midwest, the East, and the far West. There is no open range in most states. The challenge is keeping walls and fences repaired after damage by angry bulls, careless hunters, rust, and the unseen nibbling by underground pests.

The simple rail fences of pioneer times are just decorative touches today. These lumber-intensive fences, long after the great forests have disappeared, have been replaced mostly by wire and barbed wire strung between locust posts. The many styles of twisting pointed barbs on plain fence wire have created new antiques. Even a few inches of rare antique barbed wire is a much sought after treasure to the serious collector.

The fences of this farm differed from area to area. Near the house, the horizontal board fences and gates were painted white to match the house. Down at the barn, the board fences sported the same weathered grey as the barn siding. The chicken yard had a higher fence of woven wire squares to discourage ambitious hens who envied other birds that could really fly. The field fences had wooden posts strung with wires.

Some fences also had one strand of barbed wire at the top. These were in field locations where farm animals or deer might try to crush the fence in order to enter the next field of ripe soybeans or corn. An unwelcome visitor hidden in a corn field can do a lot of damage overnight.

Sometimes we kids would "help" inspect and mend the fences with Granddaddy. Walking along the fences in the farthest fields and the woods revealed that the farm was surrounded by dirt roads unnoticed from the house by us because some lacked telephone poles to mark them.

Most of the distant fences were in good shape. A few rusted-out patches, loose wire escaping from split posts, or more obvious damage by a stray car or eager hunters could be seen occasionally. The wood lot was posted for NO HUNTING followed by all that small legal wording, but hunters came and went easily. Most were fellow farmers out briefly for some sport. Only when town or city hunters were numerous was it necessary for farmers to paint large letters on their stock, COW, to avoid slaughter by over-eager trigger fingers.

There were no stone walls on this farm. Ohio soil was not stone free by any means, but there weren't the endless stones of New England begging to be used.

The breaks in the fences were examined and small repairs were made on the spot with the few hand tools Granddaddy had tucked in the many pockets of his overalls. Major breaks were remembered and had to be repaired later. For the most part, fences held up very well for years and our inspection tours turned out to be a time to be together, learn about land management and nature. "What weed is that?" "Oh, that's common milkweed. See, here, I'll show you the milk." White liquid oozed from the broken stem.

The ambling pace of grandfather and young grandchild legs made all strides fit perfectly. The frequent stops for fence work or general observation meant that we both enjoyed a few hours of easy work and good company outdoors yet we were back early enough to avoid the cows crowding down the lane ready to be milked – again.

The Indian Mound

The view from the front porch of the farmhouse reinforced the feeling we had of peace and plenty when at the farm – calm and quiet with only isolated pockets of activity. The city was the opposite, all noise and bustle with only infrequent islands of calm – a park, a pond, or a city estate with extra trees. Here, next to the comfortable front porch chairs with flowered covers, was the cobble stone railing, more like a concrete-capped broad stone wall, that served as both seat and table on occasion. Ahead, a clipped lawn separated flower garden from house. This was not a landscaped creation, but a no-nonsense narrow cutting garden. Aunt Dorothy and Grandmother planted the garden with an array of vivid blossoms attended to in long rows from the lane clear past the front porch to the old orchard out back. We could not name all of the flowers, but there were roses, poppies, daises, and a showy variety of colorful gladiolas – good bouquet flowers, firm and long lasting.

Next came the front field with its lone sugar maple right at the center. Beyond, rose the tree tops and roofs of the neighbor's farm across the county road, but a slight glance to the left revealed the Indian mound. Disguised as a swelling hill, planted with corn, then oats or wheat in another year, it seemed to be just part of the vista of the next farm.

In the early part of the 1900s, curiosity led to the mound being opened. This part of Ohio was ancient war territory and every farmer around has a collection of Indian artifacts – not excavated, but plowed up during the routine of farming. We each had been given arrowheads at different times; pink tiny ones for hunting birds or fish, others larger black flints, even polished skinning stones as beautiful and simple as modern sculpture. Later, we were to learn of their antiquity from experts; a few flints dating back thousands of years.

The legend of the hill as burial mound had been handed down for generations. Finally, the decision was made to open it and see who and what was in there. Hardly a scientific, cautious dig by archeologists, the mound surface was opened with a mechanical steam shovel initially and then more cautiously by hand tools. They say that within the burial chamber sat three chiefs, facing each other. There were numerous native artifacts surrounding the chiefs, but they were not itemized for our young ears.

One detail was told about a sealed clay pot containing "war paint." One farmer smeared some on his hand and could not get it off with any modern solvent or scouring power. It simply had to wear off months later.

The Indian mound was carefully resealed and the hill top restored. No farmer can give up a field; land is too valuable. Since then, decades of farming have reduced its profile some so that it looks today more like a low natural hill, still protecting its solemn contents within.

Deep Woods

Open fields and pastures spread out from the centrally located farmhouse and barn; the nerve centers for all rural activity. One corner of the 160 acres loomed up, a dense texture of tall trees, a remnant from pioneer days when trees covered everything before fields were cleared by sturdy axes, year after year.

We remember the bare branches of tangled grey in winter, delicate leaves in spring (not nearly as green as the winter wheat) and then the vivid colors in fall. The deep woods beckoned us because its leafy look was at once familiar, and yet its contents strangely mysterious.

When we were small, we were never allowed to venture beyond house and barn. As we grew up, the woods became the first place that we could go as a group of excited kids accompanied by Tricksey, the farm dog. Tricksey was a well-tempered, cheerful terrier that had begun life as our cousin's pet. Like so many lively puppies, she soon outgrew the back yard – and the patience of the parents. She was relocated to this farm where cousins Margaret and Joan visited many weekends. Fifteen miles to see relatives – and your pet – was not too much of a trip. Tricksey went with us to the woods to protect us from any unlikely loose cows, stray foxes, and wild dogs or, we hoped, mythical beasts.

Being able to climb easily over the gate to the lane leading to the woods meant that we were big enough to join fellow adventurers. At the end of the last fenced field, the woods suddenly began. Huge trees and bushes, strange plants close to the ground all clustered together in an area similar in size to a field, about one-sixth of the total property.

Venturing into the jumble of tree trunks supporting a leafy canopy, we were greeted with a blast of cool air, moist and dust-free – unlike the hot, shadeless journey up the lane. We relished every changing vista and textured tree trunk. Here, a giant beech tree with its grey bark trunk as wide as our dining room table. Beyond, a flicker of white dogwood blossoms, the jewelry of the woods. The whole place was enchanting, reminding us of Robin Hood or the dwarfs' or witches' woods. No gnomes dwelt here, but we looked for them anyway. We could not understand why the grownups never wanted to go to the woods. "Oh, you children go on. We have things to do."

Several times we all had picnics in the woods. Great preparations attended this exodus from kitchen to rusted grill and weathered picnic table located deep into the woods. All of the usual goodies as well as oil cloth tablecloth and picnic flatware made the trek to the best spot in the woods: a mossy, almost level area that caught flickering sunlight and where a small cooking fire would not endanger the whole place.

A special treat awaited the corn roast. Ears of corn with their husks on were soaked and buried wet on top of glowing coals in a pit. Covered with dirt, the corn slowly steamed while the picnic was readied. The special green and smoky flavor of the roasting ears was unique and became the signature flavor of those outings.

One picnic celebrated the local air races. The little airport for light planes was on the main road to town, not far from the farm. It had no paved runway, but mowed grass allowed the little private planes, some with double wings, to fling themselves into the air just short of running into the highway. A colorful windsock by the highway marked the airfield edge.

At the border of "our" woods was the skeleton of a giant tree, long dead, but still standing. The air races used this tree as a pylon above which fliers had to circle back for another leg of the race course. Several laps equaled one race.

We sat in folding chairs or on the ground and marveled at how close and how fast the colorful planes seemed to zoom around the pylon tree. It made that picnic extra special. Even grandmother obviously enjoyed the races more than we kids expected. Privately, we learned from others that our grandmother was a great fan of horse racing in earlier days. We couldn't imagine our jolly grandmother evil enough to enjoy the ponies, nor younger than she was, but the truth was out.

On one expedition deep into the woods, I stumbled upon some bones and a horse skull. The adults knew they were there, but I was startled to see death among so much lively greenery. It was Prince, the horse that years ago faithfully took our mother and her brothers to the local school and back. In winter, Prince pulled the sleigh and more than once after school he bolted up the lane to the barn. Hungry and bored, he would dump pupils and books out of the overturned sleigh on the sharp turn into the lane and plow through the deep snow, dragging the sleigh behind and heading for the warmth of his barn. The trudge up the lane with soaked books and clothes did not endear Prince to my mother and our uncles.

The horse skull was lugged from the woods, burlap bagged and taken to our suburban home where it was forced to reside in the garage.

To me, this artifact was, in my mind, a tribute to Georgia O'Keeffe and her skull and rose painting, but to my mother, it was a dirty horse skull. O'Keeffe's skulls had been bleached white by the desert sun. Prince was mellow in leaf mold. Or maybe it was the disturbed remains of a faithful, yet ornery, friend from her school days that bothered mother.

Once in awhile, a cow would get through the pasture fence and head for the woods to eat special weedy treats. The cow was herded back, the fence repaired, but eventually the woods was used as pasture and that signaled its sure end. The young tender shoots from acorns and seeds were gobbled up by the cows, and future trees never appeared.

At the end, but not while we were growing up, the woods became a stark graveyard of bleached tree trunks and fallen timber. No leafy canopy, just tree bones gleaming in the hot sun. Now the whole farm edged towards becoming one flat plane. A few trees remained, but never enough to qualify as real woods. Across the farm, crops were always rotated every year from planted field to fallow field, pigs and sheep came and went, but we always thought of "our woods" as never changing from the shady playground that we remembered and so enjoyed exploring over the years.

Beyond what is left of the woods, the rows of roof tops of expanding suburbia loom. Lots have been cut out of neighboring farms by developers. Across the road, the Indian mound on the Amish blacksmith's land has been plowed down still lower to a knoll. The steeply banked curves of the area roads have been eased a bit and paved instead of oiled and graded annually. Each farm has a house number; the anonymous entry road is a numbered county road to help firemen and postmen. But the air is still fresh and at sunset, a distant cow moos as milk house lights blink on.

The shrinking countryside survives.

After Word

The stories and characters of this slim book are true, and no names have been changed to protect the guilty. Here was a time when corporation farms were little known, horses far outnumbered tractors, level highways were only out West, and city and farm were worlds apart. In the 1930s and '40s, technology continued to overtake every aspect of world and home in that century that shrunk the globe, visited our Moon, photographed Saturn, and utilized the new electronic universe. All of this as remembered mostly through the eyes of young Ed, siblings, and cousins – recalled here decades later.

Mother	(Blanche) Mrs. Edward A. Fisher
Dad	(Ted) Edward A. Fisher, Sr.
Barbara	(Sister) Mrs. Robert D. Kelso
Ed	(Author) Ed Fisher, Jr.
Dick	(Brother) Richard W. Fisher
Grandmother	(Emma) Mrs.Delbert E.VanTilburg
Grandfather	(Del) H. Delbert VanTilburg
Aunt Dorothy	(Dorothy) Mrs Frank B. VanTilburg
Uncle Frank	Frank B. VanTilburg
Bill	(Cousin) William D. VanTilburg
Aunt Fern	Mrs. Curtis L. VanTiburg
Uncle Curt	Curtis L. VanTilburg
Margaret	(Cousin) Mrs. Robert T. Scott
Joan	(Cousin) Mrs. C. E. (Bud) Morris
June	Mrs. William D. VanTilburg
Aunt Bea	(Bea) Mrs. Edwin Balyeat

The farm mentioned here is a "quarter section" 160 acres near Ashland, Ohio where we kids loved to visit a half century ago. Still farmed, but by neighbors of Bill, now a lawyer who with his family lives close by. The rest of us are scattered across Arizona, Alabama, Michigan, and the state of the author, Pennsylvania, where he is at his final rest in the Veterans' Cemetery near Pittsburgh.

Epilogue
More About Ed

E d took great delight in writing these remembrances for family members and friends many of whom visited the VanTilburg farm and enjoyed the country side as a dramatic change from city life.

Among his many talents, he enjoyed writing. He had a fertile mind that produced more ideas and projects than could ever be completed in one lifetime. As an artist, he visualized the world and its contents differently than most people. From those visions, he maintained an ongoing list of future projects which he hoped to complete. Two of those were several children books and a stylish two foot long paper alphabet formed from laser cut letters.

His artistic abilities were well known in the Pittsburgh area and he often was sidetracked from his personal interests to respond to requests from friends and organizations for his talents. He taught 19 art-related courses for adults including creativity, water color painting and calligraphy. He enjoyed sketching and carried a sketch pad with him. Wherever he traveled he would record the scenes around him with pen and ink.

Ed retired from Carnegie Mellon University's Design Department in 1988 after twenty-three years of teaching graphic design, typography, and creativity. He designed 110 issues of Carnegie Magazine for the Carnegie Musems. He designed advertising, annual reports, as well as exhibits, commercial interiors, and provided design consultation for many organizations. He was the architect for four buildings plus some remodeling projects. Earlier, he taught at Syracuse University, was a book and magazine designer which prompted his interest in writing. As a final tribute to his talents, following is a short story written by Ed about a friend of his that he met at church. Following that is an article written by one of Ed's friends published in the newsletter of The Academy for Lifelong Learning, a Carnegie Mellon University publication.

Ed will be missed by us all.

Dick Fisher

THE 99¢ LADY by Ed Fisher

The handicapped tag comes out of the glove compartment and now hangs dutifully behind the rear view mirror of her car. Claire always feels a touch guilty about using it; she isn't really handicapped. but her even-older ladies that she shops for are---one in a walker and another elderly with a limp. They frequently come along with her to get some air and exercise, as well as to socialize in the supermarket. Strangers like to chat with them. No threat to anyone, I guess.

But today, she is alone, just shopping for Vera, her housebound 94-year-old steady customer. That's why she keeps the old automatic Buick. She'd been offered a newer, smaller car but refused, all that shifting that she hadn't done for years, and she needs a big trunk when shopping for others. It would help her now if her son would take out those snow tires, still in the trunk from last winter.

Claire slams the car door shut, twice. These old two-doors can be stubborn. On her way up the ramp into the store she rummages through her spacious leather purse of many compartments for all the clipped newspaper coupons and the list. Not bad this week. Bananas 25¢ a pound, sirloin tip roast: buy one get one free with a coupon; Klondike ice cream bars the same, canned beets on special, but zucchinis are more than at Dom and Frank's little grocery. She'll go there for them later.

Claire is in her shopping outfit, casual, but clean and colorful. Her ample grey hair is piled up in its usual bun in back, to cover her flat spot, she always says. Red jacket that matches her lipstick—a sparkle pin—tan slacks, no stockings, white tennis shoes for easy walking, all given to her when Evelyn died. I'll never have to buy any clothes; they gave me so many of her things I'll never have to shop, she reminds everyone whenever the subject of new clothes comes up.

Picking out a shopping cart, she rolls forward with a big smile past the checkout girls. They all know her. She shops in there nearly every day for someone. Bins of savory fruits in a rainbow of tropical colors beckon, as do the leafy greens spread glistening under a refreshing water spray. She wheels by. Now to the bananas, fairly green, but they ripen fast. A bunch of six nestle in the spartan cart. One item checked off. Down the next aisle for Italian bread. $1.49—imagine! she muses. I'll wait to get my own when it's 99¢. I'm the 99¢ Lady. Nearly everything goes on sale eventually for 99¢. At the end of the aisle lurks the forbidden treat: four squares of creamy cheese cake from the store's own bakery, better than Sara Lee's. It's featured in the wall case with special order cakes, spotlighted, $1.99. She looks, almost sighs, but doesn't buy. Cheese cake must be reserved for birthdays and such.

The shopping continues, item by item. Vera has listed every choice in a surprisingly firm hand, ordering each size, brand, and price. Vera is particular about brands. Well, so is Claire, who will eat only French vanilla from King's; her divorced son will eat only regular vanilla, always. That means two ice creams in one refrigerator. Vera wants Foodland beets, sliced. They're on special. Never get her another brand, it's dangerous. Next, the applesauce. Has to be the big jars, 48 ounces, Motts, three of them. How she can eat so much applesauce no one knows, but she does. And Swanson's frozen dinners, four for $7 this week. Vera wants 12, three each of four kinds—Veal Parmesan becomes the hardest to find in the fogged-up case. Claire hates frozen dinners, never serves them.

She cooks everything from scratch, including mashed potatoes—only Idahos—which her retired daughter then finishes with extra milk, and more butter—not margarine—than either one of them needs to eat. Claire has cooked her "famous" spaghetti and meatballs for years for family and friends. Each batch is analyzed. Is it as good as last time? Spicier, milder, could be hotter, the spaghetti was overcooked, better ground meat this time, etc. Always fresh; she won't ever use that powdered stuff. Claire and garlic are inseparable. She puts it in everything. Maybe that is what keeps her face so smooth and youthful. Garlic, she insists, and cold cream. Water hasn't touched that face for years. Woody, the postman, even gets a spaghetti sample on spaghetti day along with his ever-present mug of ice water that each day balances on the brick window ledge next to the flag. Claire often flies the flag. Her late, very late, husband was in the military.

Three aisles later, the shopping is nearly done. The cart bulges with the last purchases piled on top. One quart of regular vitamin

D, not skim, not 2%, but regular milk. Vera's slim as a rail, so milk fat is fine. And some yogurt. Claire hates yogurt, even frozen yogurt, and wonders how Vera can stomach that mushy stuff. Then race pass the prepared foods and Deli counter. The steaming chicken and gravy feast the air. Nothing to get there. The specialty at that counter, a crispy fried fish sandwich on a Kaiser bun tantalizes every Friday. Not today, of course.

The checkout ritual is a gab fest, an exchange of personal moments, news of relatives, and comments delivered like a movie review about the store's contents and prices. The applesauce becomes a challenge. Keep the packers from putting all three jars in one bag; too much weight for Claire. Why do they do that? she wonders. Change from Vera's hundred is put in a special pouch in her purse along with the trailing ribbon of sales slip. Vera did save nearly $11 from coupons and specials. Some weeks the newspaper has a whole page of great specials. Today, Vera is getting every brand that she expected.

The groceries travel to Vera's tiny house. Only a few shallow steps to the front door and all travels to the kitchen. She sorts things out to the refrigerator and freezer or to shelves. Claire loosens the tight applesauce lids for her. The grocery bags are folded and filed. That's done. Now to make it home in time take Dolly to the hospital to visit her son. Then Alice has to be taken to Bingo at seven: it's Tuesday. Just down the road, but Claire knows that the 99¢ Lady has to keep moving. She sallies forth from job to job grabbing a bite of leftovers before fixing a big pan of her "famous" Swedish meatballs and noodles for her two children at home.

Remembering Ed Fisher

Our friendship began at the Academy for LifeLong Learning (A.L.L.) almost ten years ago. My special interest was in taking classes. Ed was always a study leader, committee chair, board member, and all-around problem solver. Somehow we were drafted into serving on the Special Events Committee to plan "one-day" events. Most of the ideas emanated from Ed's fertile brain (and most of the details were left to me).

We were a great team. Ed never lacked for trip suggestions throughout Western Pennsylvania, Ohio, and West Virginia. He even completed maps on how to get there. We have enough ideas for the rest of the century. We had fun planning and sometimes would do dry runs to see if the places were as interesting as they sounded and if there were other points of interest nearby. Once we settled on a destination, Ed would prepare those provocative flyers, and we never lacked for A.L.L. enrollees. Frequently we were oversubscribed.

I was always in awe of Ed's many talents—his graphic artistry is legendary for the flyers announcing the events, but his writing was equally creative when he described the event and when he would write about the happening afterwards.

And, so, sadly a number of A.L.L. members joined his family, friends and church members at his memorial service on Saturday, January 27, 2007 at the First Church of Christ, Scientist in Wilkinsburg. There we saw the abundant display of his paintings in the Reading Room and the whimsical, colorful ones in the nursery.

While losing him was sad, his legacy of paintings, graphics, and memories reflect his droll humor and the many acts of kindness for which he'll be remembered. Goodbye, old friend. If anyone deserves an honored place in heaven, you do.

Bob Dickman

Colophon

This first edition has been sponsored by Dick Fisher, who also computer set the manuscript in 12 point Shruti and headings in 16 point Rockwell. Pen and ink sketches are by the author. Printing and binding by Trafford Publishing, Canada.